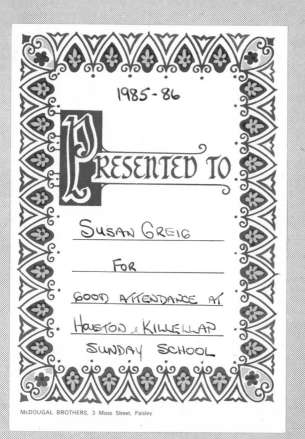

1985-86

PRESENTED TO

Susan Greig

For

Good Attendance at

Houston & Killellan

Sunday School

McDOUGAL BROTHERS, 3 Moss Street, Paisley

Best Loved Stories

LORNA DOONE

by R. D. Blackmore

Abridged edition

Elements of Education

I, John Ridd, of the parish of Oare in the county of Somerset, yeoman and churchwarden, have seen and had a share in some doings of this neighbourhood, which I will try to set down in order. My father sent me to school in Tiverton, in Devon, but I was called away from it at the age of twelve. On the 29th day of November, 1673, the very day when I was twelve years old, John Fry, who worked for my father, came to the school to fetch me home, although he would not tell me why.

From Tiverton to the town of Oare is a very long and painful road, and John Fry and I lodged in inns on the way. At Dulverton a foreign lady's maid asked me to pump water for her in the yard, and this I did, much embarrassed. On the road out of Dulverton I saw her again, for she was in the front of a large coach pulled by six horses. By her side was a little girl, dark-haired and very beautiful, but in the honourable place sat another lady who looked very noble. There was another child by her side, a boy, two or three years old with a white cockade in his hat. His mother looked at us very kindly, but when I asked John Fry who they were he would say only that they were "murdering Papishers" and little he cared to do with them, or the devil they came from.

After that the road got worse and worse until there was none at all, and the fog came down upon the moors as thick as I ever saw it, and there was no sound or breath of wind. There were little stubby trees here and there, which were dripping with wet, and soon it grew too dark to see anything at all.

But now we had to keep very quiet, for we were near to the Doone track, two miles from Dunkery Beacon hill, the highest place on Exmoor. I knew at once whom he meant — those bloody Doones of Bagworthy, the awe of all Devon and Somerset, outlaws, traitors, murderers, and if they should be abroad tonight we had better lie low.

John Fry was sure that they could see through any thickness of fog, and he insisted that we continued on our way in the hollow ground, away from the Doone-track.

It was as well that we did, for very soon we heard horses coming along behind us, and a light flared as someone set fire to the Beacon, to guide the Doones home. There were more than thirty of them, heavy men and large of stature, with guns, swords and armour. Some had carcasses of sheep, others deer, all had plunder behind their saddles and flagons of ale or wine in front, and one of them had a child flung across his saddle bow. I could not see if the child were alive or dead, for it was flung across head downwards, and it was very young. Its dress shone bright with gold and jewels, which was probably the reason for its capture. I was so enraged to see that poor child among those vultures that I shouted at them, leaping on a rock and raving at them. Two of them turned round and one pointed his gun at me,

8

but the other said I was a pixie and that they'd be better off keeping their powder. Little did they know, thought I, that one day that pixie would dance down their castle.

John Fry was very angry, and said it was no thanks to me that his new wife wasn't now a widow, but I said nothing at all. We rejoined the homeward road, and set off once again, and it was not long before we arrived at my father's farm. He did not come out to greet me, and indeed the place seemed wholly silent until I heard the sound of my mother and sisters weeping, and realised that my father was dead.

A Rash Visit

My dear father had been killed by the Doones of Bagworthy while riding home from Porlock market on Saturday evening. With him were six other very sober farmers, and they were all singing hymns and psalms to keep their courage up when one of the Doones stopped in the starlight full across them. They knew who he was at once, and although it seemed like one man against seven, it was in fact one against one, for the other six farmers were of the type that would merely hand over their money to a Doone.

But my father was made of sterner stuff, and he raised his stick and rode at the Doone robber, who made his escape. Suddenly my father was in the middle of a dozen men, but his courage did not fail him and he laid about him with his stick until a man beyond his reach killed my father with a long gun. Next morning his body was found on the moors, with his stick broken under him.

My mother was full of sorrow at her loss, but in those days it was no rare thing to become a widow. She had three children — myself, my sister Annie was next, with about two years between us, and next came little Eliza. Before I arrived home, my mother had paid a visit to the Doones. They had met her on the moors and had blindfolded her until they reached the cottages where the Doones lived. Two men led my mother to the house where the captain lived, Sir Ensor Doone, and although he seemed very charming and courteous, he did not help her at all. She found that it was Carver Doone who had killed my father, and the Doones said that he was killed in self-defence — a tale of atrocious lies. While she was on her way home again, a Doone came up behind her and offered her a bag of money. Her pride rebelled, and she dropped it on the ground. She would not accept money or pity from a family whose founder, Sir Ensor, had been outlawed back in 1640, and whose very name caused nightmares.

Over that winter, I learned how to shoot my father's gun, and then on St Valentine's Day, 1675, I went fishing in the Lowman river. At first I was not successful, but then I came upon a great black pit of

water, with a swift torrent rushing down into it, and I stepped in, losing my balance and almost being drowned. After some struggling, I climbed out, and fell unconscious on the bank.

When I came to myself, there was a little girl hanging over me, with soft black hair and eyes, rich clothes and the prettiest voice I ever heard. She was much concerned over me, and was aghast at my wet state.

"How you are looking at me!" I said. "My name is John Ridd. What is your name?"

"Lorna Doone," she said in a low voice, as if afraid of it, and began to cry. I comforted her as best I could, and was taken aback when she flung her little arms round my neck and kissed me. Then I felt ashamed, for she was far better born than I — the Doones were related to lords, and I was but a yeoman's boy.

Then she warned me to go, for fear the Doones, who would be looking for her, would kill me if they found me, and that I could well believe. I ran away as fast as I could, then hid myself some way away and watched. A dozen fierce men were walking towards us, and calling for the "queen", as they named her. Lorna lay down and pretended to be asleep. They found her very soon. Then one of the great rough men picked her up and kissed her, and I wished I had my father's gun with me.

"Here's our queen!" he shouted, and hoisted her on to his shoulders. "Here's the captain's daughter."

Then they all strode away, until they reached a darkened glen, when Lorna turned slightly and raised her hand to me.

Cousin Tom

One November evening when I was about fifteen years old our cousin Tom Faggus, the highwayman, visited us. He was a very famous man, and caused us much merriment and happiness by his presence. My mother wept to see him, which surprised me for I had long since ceased to weep for the death of my father, and Cousin Tom said fiercely to her, "I am in some ways a bad man, but I know the value of a good one — and if you give me orders — by God —" And he shook his fist towards Bagworthy Wood.

"Hush, Tom, hush, for goodness sake," said my mother hastily, and I knew that although she did not point towards me, she meant me. For she had ever weaned me from thoughts of revenge, saying that God knew best about judgment and retribution.

The Doones were thriving still, although complaints were made against them from time to time. Some folk said that I, being grown enough, should do something about the Doones, and show what I was made of, but I saw no point in killing one of them. If I had met the man who killed my father, I would have thrashed him black and blue, but I would not have killed him.

It happened when I was twenty one, that my mother's uncle, Master Reuben Huckaback of Dulverton, came to visit us on New Year's Eve. We were to have dinner at one o'clock, and supper at six, but Master Huckaback did not arrive, and my mother feared that the Doones had caught him. They had indeed, and being good Catholics, had indulged too much in alcohol, so that they had done him no harm, but created much mischief by tying him to his old nag and chasing him about Exmoor. They had also robbed him. I set off to find him, and soon did so, as he was lamenting the fate which had robbed him after a peaceful life of sixty five years.

Uncle Ben was so angered by the robbery that he attempted to bring the justices on to the Doones, but when this failed he was very angry and told me that he would speak to one higher than they — Judge Jeffreys, but that he would not see him until the summer for he could not go to London on purpose.

While escorting Uncle Ben through Bagworthy Wood, I caught sight of Lorna Doone again.

At first she pretended not to know me, and was very haughty, and I remembered that the Doones, although outlaws, were of high birth, and I was but a yeoman. But then Lorna spoke pleasantly to me, warning me of the dangers of the Doones finding me in that place and begging me to go before I came to harm. I did as she told me, and for the homeward journey was mad with every man in the world who would dare to think of looking at her.

John is Bewitched

I myself can never know how I loved my Lorna. That week I could do little more than dream and dream, and wonder how soon I ought to go again upon a visit to Glen Doone. It seemed bad manners to me to go back without being invited, and besides the weather had chapped my hands and face so much that she might have thought me ugly.

When the weather changed and the frost was gone it was more than I could do to keep from thought of Lorna. I went up there one day, and was so happy at the thought that I might see her, that I fell asleep in a bed of moss. I woke when Lorna herself stood between me and the light of the sun.

"Master Ridd, are you mad?" she said. "The patrol will be here directly. Let me hide you."

I followed her to her secret room, a cave within the rocks, carpeted with moss and with a spring rising in its centre, and there, after I had persuaded her to call me John instead of Master Ridd, she told me her story.

She was the granddaughter of Sir Ensor Doone, the daughter of his eldest son of whom she had no remembrance. Sir Ensor was one of only two Doones to listen and care for her — the other being a man they called the Counsellor, one known as a wise man. All around her had been violence and robbery, coarse delight and savage pain. Then she spoke of Carver Doone, who had slain my father.

15

She told me that for strength and courage he bore the first repute among the Doones, being the Counsellor's son. But he was very hot and savage and beyond argument and reason.

The one person she cared for was her maid, a Cornish girl called Gwenny Carfax, whose father was a miner in a Cornish tin mine, and who vanished, never to be seen again. Lorna had saved Gwenny from starving, and was repaid with her devotion.

About a year before, something strange had happened while she was walking. A strange young man had appeared before her, knowing who she was and claiming that he was her guardian according to Scottish law. His name was Lord Alan Brandir,

and he said he was her cousin, and just as he was leaving her, he was caught by the massive figure of Carver Doone and carried off. She never saw the young man again — but afterwards she saw Carver smoking a cigar very like Alan Brandir's. Here she stopped, unable to tell more, and wept for very fear.

Lorna and I agreed that I would not go to Glen Doone for another month, unless she gave a sign that my help was needed, which was that she would throw a dark covering over a white stone in the entrance to the cave. I rode home, sad and weary, and on my return found young Marwood de Whichehalse, the son of our local Baron, flirting with my sister Annie, who did not know how to scold him. I clouted him soundly about the head and left him lying there, and was surprised some days later to receive a letter of apology from Marwood himself, not only addressed to me but to Annie too, at which I soon forgave him.

A Royal Invitation

Soon after this we had a visitor, whom I invited in for some supper and ale. He was looking for me, and delivered to me a summons to appear before the King's Bench in Westminster, where I was to deliver such evidence as I could about the keeping of King Charles's peace in Somerset. The messenger, Jeremy Stickles, and I were not to depart for London until the next Saturday. My mother was sure that I would have great honours heaped upon my head, but I was worried because of my Lorna. What would she think if she needed me and I had gone? But there was nothing I could do about it.

I was in London for two full months before I saw the justices, and had spent the last of the money that my mother had given me. But at last I was admitted into the presence of Judge Jeffreys, the Lord Chief Justice.

He asked me about the Doones, and I told him all I knew, and then he inquired after the family of de Whichehalse, and whether I thought the two families were in league. This idea was so new to me that it set my wits all wandering, and the judge saw this. He bade me stay clear of the Doones, of the de Whichehalses, and to advise my cousin Tom Faggus, whom he knew of old, to mend his ways before he was hanged.

It was the beginning of the harvest when I arrived home. My mother, Annie and Lizzie were overjoyed to see me again, and much as I longed to know more about Lorna, I could not leave them yet on the following day, which was a Sunday.

But on the Monday I went to see her, and found that she had needed me over two months before when I had not been there. I told her I loved her, and she admitted to liking me, but no more. I knew she was a prize coveted by Carver Doone, and by a gallant young man called Charleworth Doone, and I hated them both for it.

I gave her a ring I had brought her from London, sapphires with pearls, but Lorna refused to take it until she loved me properly, and with that I had to be content.

Lorna forbade me to see her again for two months, during which time we brought in the harvest, and I confided in Annie about Lorna, and she in me about Tom Faggus wishing to marry her, although she said she would not do it until I was wed. My uncle Reuben Huckaback visited us at harvest time, and with him his granddaughter Ruth, a tiny little girl whom I mistook for a child, although she was all of seventeen. Annie danced with Squire Marwood de Whichehalse, and my mother saw the two couples together and beamed, little dreaming how her schemes would be upset!

Uncle Reuben showed no desire to leave us at once. He took to riding alone beyond our parish, and I sent John Fry after him, and John Fry told us that he had seen him going near to the Wizard's Slough, a terrible bog as black as death, the worst quagmire on the whole of Exmoor. There was a tale that it was here that murderers came to life again, and in the gathering darkness John Fry saw a human shape rise out of the pit, or so he thought. So frightened was he that he rode straight home again.

Carver Doone

I thought long upon John Fry's story, and the more I thought the more uneasy I became, especially following on the warning of Judge Jeffreys. I knew that there was much dissatisfaction with the king, and regret for the days of the Puritans. But was it likely that Master Reuben Huckaback, a wealthy man and a careful one, would have anything to do with it?

And what about the Doones themselves? They were not likely to entertain much affection for a king whose father had outlawed them and taken their property.

I was much worried and perplexed about this, but before I had decided what to do, Uncle Reuben left as suddenly as he had come, leaving his granddaughter Ruth with us until he could safely fetch her back to Dulverton.

As soon as the eight weeks of my two months' ban from Lorna were over, I went up once more to see if I could find her. I took her some eggs and the pearl ring, hoping that this time she would accept it. But instead the huge figure of Carver Doone came into the valley. He was not an ugly man — indeed rather handsome, but there was something in his face which turned one cold. There was no curve in his face of weakness, or of afterthought, of playfulness or pleasantry. He looked as though he knew nothing of smiling, and his blue eyes were like steel.

Finding my eggs for Lorna, Carver smiled, believing that Charleworth Doone had put them there. He had obviously been robbing the Counsellor's henhouse. Carver picked up the eggs and walked away with them, and I stayed where I was — better to do so than to allow him to discover who Lorna met there, since he and the Doones wished her to marry him.

I waited, but there was no sign of Lorna, so wearily I returned to the farm.

I returned there early the next morning, and to my delight I saw Lorna coming towards me. For a while she talked of other things than the one I wished to know, but at last she told me that she loved me. I was overjoyed, and slipped the pearl ring onto her wedding finger. This time she kept it, and clung to me with fondness and a flood of tears. I comforted her as best I could, but she murmured, "It can never, never be. Who am I to dream of it? Something in my heart tells me so, it can never be, never."

When I returned home, I found Tom Faggus, or Squire Faggus, as everyone now called him, having breakfast with my mother and sisters. On going out to sow some grass seed, he refused to come with me, and instead stayed and asked my mother for Annie's hand in marriage. I returned to find everyone in a rare taking. So I took Annie and Mother on one side and I told Mother about Lorna. Annie already knew about it. Then we spoke of Tom Faggus, and assured Mother that she would never be turned out into the street by her children. At last, after many tears, which she seemed to enjoy shedding, my mother said she was an old fool, and gave her consent to our two marriages.

Ruth is Not Like Lorna

My mother was greatly worried when she learned that I was risking my life, as she saw it, every time I saw Lorna, and put her mind to save me further danger and her more worry.

"And of one thing I am glad," she said. "That Uncle Reuben called my boy a coward because he would not lead an action into the valley that shelters his beloved one! All the time this dreadful 'coward' is risking his life daily there, without a word to anyone! How glad I am that you will not have, for all her miserable money, that little dwarfish granddaughter of the old miser!"

She turned as she said it, and saw Ruth herself standing just beside her. Ruth tried to answer her with some spirit, but then broke down completely, and ran from the room. I admired her then for her spirit, and my mother too.

"I shall beg her pardon," she said, "before she goes." For Ruth had said that she would be returning to Dulverton as soon as possible.

The next time I saw Lorna, she gave me a ring in return for her own.

"Look at it," she said. "What a queer old thing! It was on the front of my old glass necklace."

I asked her about the glass necklace, and she answered that she had worn it in her childhood, and did not know where it had come from, but she remembered that her grandfather had begged her to

give it to him for safe keeping when she was about ten years old, but he had given her back the ring and told her to keep it safe and be proud of it. And so she had done, and now it became John Ridd's delight.

After we had celebrated Allhallows and the eve of Fawkes, we had a visitor in the shape of Jeremy Stickles, the king's messenger, who had come to our neighbourhood to make enquiries about possible risings. He told me about the Duke of Monmouth, the king's illegitimate son, who had been banished because he wished to be king after his father's death, instead of his uncle, the king's brother James, the Duke of York. Jeremy Stickles was in Somerset to watch the gathering of a secret plot, not so much against the king as against the lawful succession to his throne. He warned me to stick to the winning side, which I would willingly do if I knew which that were.

After that, my own affairs were thrown into much disorder, for suddenly without any warning, all of Lorna's signals ceased. Three times I went up to the valley where we met, but there was no sign of her. I even went down into the valley where the Doones lived, finding Carver's cottage deserted, which I rejoiced at, for I had dreaded to find Lorna there. At last I returned to the farm, resolving to return to Glen Doone and learn what had happened to my Lorna.

I went there the very next night, and made my stealthy way down into Glen Doone, to the robbers' township. There were two guards only, and both of them were drunk. From their conversation I learned that Lorna was still at her grandfather's house, that she had not been given to Carver as his bride, and for this I was very thankful.

I followed one of the guards, whom I knew to be Charleworth or Charlie Doone, who was going to report to Carver, the captain that night. As we passed Sir Ensor's dwelling, I saw Charleworth glance upwards to where a lighted window was, and I knew that Lorna was there. The building was one storey high, and I was very close to Lorna's window, when one of the guards spotted me against the brickwork and challenged me. By chance I whistled the tune that I had heard Charleworth Doone whistling before, and to my amazement, the man fell back and saluted. I learned afterwards that I had hit upon Carver Doone's password tune, which Charleworth imitated, and the guard believed that I was that vile Carver. But he had done me the kindest service, for Lorna came to the window to see what the shouting was. Swiftly I made myself known to her and she told me that her grandfather Sir Ensor was very ill and not likely to live long. The Counsellor and Carver were in control, and neither Lorna nor little Gwenny the maid could leave the township, so they could not leave a message for me. Then Lorna bade me go as soon as possible, for fear of what might happen to me if I were caught, and told me of a plan she had to tell me if anything had happened. There was a tree with seven rooks' nests in it, right against the sides of the valley. Gwenny had often climbed the tree in the summer. I was to look at the tree daily. If I saw six nests only, Lorna was in peril and needed me. If I saw only five, she had been carried off by Carver Doone. I shuddered at the thought, and she bade me go again, and swiftly. So I left Glen Doone.

Soon after this I had cause to save Jeremy Stickles' life, when Carver and Charleworth Doone and Marwood de Whichehalse were lying in wait for him near the farm. Then, Jeremy took me into his confidence, whether I wanted it or no, about what he did in Somerset. He had three duties — to take care of the smugglers in and around the town of Lynmouth, to watch and report on every aspect of the Doones, and to learn how the people of the west country felt towards the king and to stop any attempts by those who were dissatisfied to rebel. The soldiers Jeremy had with him were very few indeed. Jeremy Stickles said that he would ask Uncle Reuben to help him in the venture, to prove his loyalty to the king — as this had been dubious lately, due to those mysterious rides close to Wizard's Slough. I had nothing to say against this, but I was afraid for the farm, for my mother, my sisters and the harvest itself, and afraid too of being called a coward by our neighbours for doing nothing against the Doones. But amongst all these troubles there was one bright spark of comfort. Tom Faggus returned from London with a royal pardon, which everyone admired the more because nobody could read a word of it.

There was one day soon after when, looking up at the rooks' nests in the tree, I could see only six – Lorna was in peril and needed me! I sat and waited for hours and hours until it grew dark, and a frost was beginning.

As the darkness gathered, Gwenny Carfax came up from the valley to fetch me. Old Sir Ensor was dying, and wished to see me before he died. Lorna had told him everything, and he could not die without speaking to me about his granddaughter. I followed Gwenny down into the valley, to where Lorna waited for me, and she led me in turn to her dying grandfather's room, leaving the two of us alone.

Sir Ensor reminded me of how low was my birth when compared to Lorna's, and forbade me to see her again. He wanted me to swear this before her, and asked me to call her in. I said nothing, but went and fetched my Lorna. We entered the room with our arms about one another, and I made Sir Ensor a low bow.

"You two fools!" he said.

"Maybe," I said, "but we are well content, as long as we are two fools together."

He paused for a long time, and seemed to soften, then he looked at us both and said, "This is the best thing I can wish you: boy and girl, be boy and girl until you have grandchildren."

Sir Ensor died soon after, but before he did so, he beckoned me to give to Lorna the glass necklace that she had had as a child.

The next day I started forth immediately for Glen Doone.

It had begun to snow again, blindingly, and this helped me somewhat for it disguised me against spying Doone eyes. At last I reached the house in the Doone township where my Lorna lived. I had arrived not a moment too soon, for the cold had almost frozen Lorna, and there was little food to be had. Lorna was faint with hunger and cold. I had brought some bread and a great pie with me, and I fed the two of them before we set out, while we waited for the snow to freeze solid, which would make our passage easier. As we waited, I saw a great red glow some way off, and Lorna told me that the Doones were setting light to Dunkery Beacon, to celebrate their new captain, Counsellor Doone. This was a great boon, for all the Doones would be very drunk in three hours' time or so, and our escape would be the easier for that.

Our journey was long and very cold, and I was afraid that the cold would kill my Lorna. But at last we arrived at the farm, and Lorna was sleeping.

Lorna slept for a long time, and I was afraid that the frost had got into her brain. But at last she awoke, and looked about her, and saw my mother. She guessed who she was, and before I could stop her she jumped up and ran to the old oak chair where Mother was pretending to be knitting, and she took Mother's hands from the work and laid them both upon her head, kneeling humbly and looking up.

"God bless you, my fair mistress," said my mother bending nearer. "God bless you, my sweet child!"

Tom Faggus Makes Some Lucky Hits

The snow lasted for a long, long time, which was to our advantage because it meant that the Doones could not come to the farm to wreak their revenge on me for stealing Carver's unwilling bride-to-be. But at last it began to rain, and there were great floods as the snow melted.

At last we had word that Tom Faggus, who had bought himself some land, would be visiting soon.

Squire Faggus made a most gallant bow, but his eyes rested for a long while on two things – Lorna's face and the old glass necklace she had round her slender neck. After we had dined, and there was only my mother, Tom Faggus and myself in the room, the squire turned to me and said abruptly, "How much do you know about that fair maiden?"

I told him as much as I knew. Tom said that he was sure that he had seen my Lorna's face before, years ago, but he could not remember where it was, or anything about it. He had never ventured into Glen Doone, and told me I was being foolish in keeping Lorna at the farm, for by so doing I was endangering not only the house and the livestock, but our own lives too.

"She has nothing," I began, but he laughed.

"The necklace, you great oaf," he said. "That necklace is worth all your farm put together, and your Uncle Ben's fortune, and all the town of Dulverton. Glass, indeed! They are the finest brilliants ever I set my eyes upon, and I have handled a good many."

That same day we told Lorna the value of her old glass necklace, and she then gave it to me for safe keeping. I kept it under my jacket, near my heart.

Scarcely was Tom Faggus out of sight than Jeremy Stickles rode up in great haste, having been

pursued by three great Doones. No men had come with him, but he had the promise of two hundred to rout out the Doones when the roads were more passable. I told him all about Lorna, and Jeremy said that we could not hope to escape an attack from the outlaws, especially now that he was there too. We began to make the entrances to the farm secure, and to keep a watch through the night. Lorna was sure that any attack that came would be on her account, but I told her that this was not so, and that if she heard anything at all during the night, she was to sleep and not on any account go to the window to see. Then she said that with all the floods, Glen Doone would probably be underwater, and that with all the trouble that it entailed, there would not be many Doones free to attack us.

We sent the girls early to bed that night, and I fell asleep myself after a while. I woke when Lorna touched me lightly on the arm. The moon was up, she said, and men could see to travel by. Gwenny had gone out to climb one of the trees and see if there was movement. I sent Lorna back to her room, and went outside. Gwenny waited for me, saying that there were ten Doones who had just crossed the water below the farm and were creeping up by the hedge. I sent her to the house to rouse Jeremy Stickles and his men, then I lay low and watched the Doones. They rode up boldly to our yard, and opened the stable doors, driving out our horses and stabling their own in their place. I was aghast at their insolence. The troopers were by now waiting in the shadow of the house, and Jeremy had made them wait before they opened fire.

They passed very close to me, and I heard Carver's cruel voice ordering his outlaws to kill every man and child and to spare the women, for Lorna was his, and my sisters were pretty enough to be carried off and become Doone women. Then two of the men began to advance on the hayrick with lighted torches. But they never fired it, for I broke the arm of one and the collar-bone of the other with tricks I had learned from wrestling.

Meanwhile, six of our men had begun to fire on the Doones, and two of the outlaws fell. I strode up to Carver Doone and took him by the beard and laid him flat upon his back in the muck of the yard. Seeing this, the others fled, some with their horses, and others – including Carver – without them. We had gained six fine horses by this, as well as two prisoner Doones and two dead ones, and I knew well that Carver Doone would never forgive or forget his humiliation that night.

Soon after, the Counsellor called at the house. I greeted him pleasantly and courteously for he was well born, like all the Doones, and Lorna greeted him too. Then the Counsellor tried to divide my Lorna and me by a number of ways – he told us that our fathers slew each other. I would not believe it, and I told him directly that Sir Ensor Doone had given his consent to our marriage. Then the

Counsellor called upon Lorna to say whether she too could dismiss the accusation as a mere trifle. Lorna was brave, and told her uncle pleasantly enough, that she knew that nine-tenths of what was spoken in Glen Doone was false, and that this was yet another example of such falsehood. Her speech was long, and she was overcome at its end and fainted away. My mother, who was extremely angry, shook her fist at the Counsellor, and was led away by my sisters. I led the Counsellor into our kitchen, and gave him some liquor and a good cigar, and we talked pleasantly enough. He told me that he had intended to come down on the farm that night, but that now he would not because I had treated him as the gentleman he was.

The Way to Make the Cream Rise

Gentleman he may have seemed, but the Counsellor was a wily one. Coming across Annie the next morning, for he had accepted my offer of hospitality, he found that she was stirring the cream, and told her that he knew an old magic trick which would make it rise twice as thick and three times the volume of what it had begun as. All that was necessary was to pass a string of clear glass beads over the top of the cream, retire to the bedroom, and recite the Lord's Prayer three times backwards. Annie, eager to make the cream rise, ran to the little place where Lorna now kept her jewels, thinking that they were safer there, and took them down to the kitchen.

"Oh, those old things," said the Counsellor with scorn when he saw them. The diamonds were passed over the cream, Annie ran up to her room to say the prayer, and the Counsellor bade a very courteous farewell to my mother and left the house. He took the diamonds with him.

The whiteness of Annie's face when she discovered the loss put the newly-whitewashed walls of the kitchen to shame. But Lorna roundly abused all diamonds, hugged Annie and my mother, and tried to comfort them as best she could, although their grief was great.

Jeremy Finds Out Something

Jeremy Stickles was much amused to hear about Annie's foolishness, but grew grave when he heard of the jewels, and said he had learned something while he was away. As he was travelling from Dulverton to Watchett, he found that he had taken a wrong turning, and that there was nothing in front of him but the sea itself. Looking about, he spotted a house with welcoming lights in the windows, and rode to it, discovering that it was an inn.

The hostess was a dark-haired, dark-eyed foreign woman, an Italian by birth, called Benita, who had gone to Rome to seek her fortune. While working in a large hotel a noble English family had arrived there. In the main they were good Catholics, but one of their number had given offence by the folly of trying to think for himself. Some bitter feud had been among them, and the sister of the nobleman who had died quite lately was married to the rival claimant whom they all detested. It was something about the division of land, but Benita did not know what.

The family offered to take her on to attend to the children and comfort the lady, and she was glad to do it. At first, the lord was as gay as could be, and would gallop in front of the carriage at a furious pace without any weapon. They journeyed through Northern Italy and France, and towards the Pyrenees, my lord riding far ahead to catch the first glimpse of a famous view, his fine young horse leaping at every step.

They waited for him a long time, but he never returned, and a week later his mangled body was lying in a chapel-yard. His lady decided that she and her family, which would be increased very shortly when she gave birth to her last child, would return to England. They landed on the Devon coast, ten or eleven years ago, and set out in a hired coach for Watchett in the north of Somerset, where the lady owned a quiet mansion.

When they reached the pitch and slope of the sea-bank they were set upon by a group of fierce-looking riders. Amid the panic that set in, the coach was all but overturned when the postillions drove it nearly into the sea, and just as it was heeling over, the lady exclaimed, "I know that man! He is our ancient enemy!"

Benita snatched the most valuable of the jewels belonging to the lady, fearing that they would all be taken by the robbers. This most valuable piece was a magnificent necklace of diamonds. This she slipped over the little girl's head, covering her with her riding cloak. Then she received a great blow upon the head and knew no more until she found herself on the sand. There was no sign of the little girl. The next day the lady died, together with the child that she bore that night, and the mother, her little son and the baby were buried in Watchett churchyard.

"But what was the lady's name?" asked I. "What became of the little girl? And why did Benita stay there, where the terrible tragedy occurred?"

"Benita stayed there," said Jeremy, "because the robbers, which I believe were all Doones, took all the valuable objects, including Benita's wages, which she could never get back because it went to Chancery in London and has stayed there ever since. They are still disputing it. She met and married a man who proved himself a good soul. The little girl —you great oaf! You are rather more likely to know than anyone else in the whole kingdom!"

"Jeremy, if I knew, I should not ask you."

"Very well. As certain sure as I stand here, that little maid is Lorna Doone."

As soon as he had said it, I began to remember

that day when John Fry and I rode past a great coach, with a little boy, a fine lady and a beautiful little girl in it. I remembered the foreign maid I had spoken to at the tavern, and I also remembered the sight of the helpless child thrown head down over the robber's saddle-bow, and my indignation at such a sight. I knew it was true.

We decided to tell Lorna nothing of this yet, for we knew nothing of her parents' names or rank, but never for one moment did I dream that she would leave me for any such reason.

There was now a new development in my Lorna's life – that the King's Court of Chancery in London heard of her life, and came to scent her out, knowing how rich she was. Upon this, and with Jeremy's permission, I told my mother all I knew about Lorna's parentage, and then we agreed that the time had come to tell Lorna herself. This I did, feeling that now she could only look at me with scorn and pity, but she did not, and I knew that whether she was countess or queen of England, mine she was at least in heart, and she was of the same opinion.

When my tale was done, she turned away and wept bitterly for the sad fate of her parents, but showed no curiosity as to her real name, and no desire to leave me and the farm for higher things. In fact, rather the opposite. She all but swore that she would not go, that she would stay in Somerset with me, and looking at her sweet face I could not help but believe it.

Not knowing how soon my Lorna would be taken to London, I rode one day to the inn of which Jeremy had spoken. I announced myself as the boy who had filled the foreign lady's glass with water all those years ago. She remembered at once, and I drew her mind back to the noble lady she had served, and the little boy who had died, and the little girl who had been stolen away. She gave me accounts of Lorna when she was five years old, and when I asked if she would know the little girl again as a full-grown maiden, she believed that she would, from looking at her eyes. Lorna's father was the Earl of Dugal.

The next morning I drove Benita to the farm, and we were met at the gate by Lorna herself. Benita and she stared at one another for a moment, and then fell into each other's arms — they had recognised each other at once, despite the changes that the years had brought.

After that there was no trouble about proving Lorna's identity, for we had the great ring that she had given me, and Benita told us that the cat and the tree on it formed the badge of the House of Lorne to which Lorna belonged, through her mother. Hot blood ran in the family, and the Doones were related to them. They had fallen out with the Earl of Lorne, after his daughter had married Sir Ensor Doone, and this had led to even more bitterness. When they had kidnapped her, the Doones had kept her safe from their gallants, keeping her ready for honourable marriage with Carver, by which much wealth would come to them, enough to buy the pardons of a thousand Doones – and the old Earl of Dugal would be very bitter at having Carver Doone as his heir.

While we were marvelling over this tale, another event took place in the family – Annie's wedding to Tom Faggus, and I rode to Dulverton to ask Uncle Reuben and Ruth if they would come to the wedding.

Uncle Reuben was not in when I arrived, but Ruth greeted me kindly, and it was not long before the old man arrived, greatly aged and shrunken since the last time I had seen him.

He took me into a private room in the house, and there asked me if I would marry Ruth, who, he said, loved me. At this I was wholly amazed at his knowledge of it, and could not say a single word, but he went on, berating me for a fool, and very spitefully calling me a knave. This was a little too much for me. Therefore, without a word, I left making only a bow to him.

He followed me however, and attempted to persuade me to marry Ruth, by asking me to listen to a secret he had to tell me. I answered carefully that I would hear anything, so long as it was legal, at which he laughed.

"Now, who, do you suppose, is at the bottom of this Exmoor insurgency, all this western rebellion – who is at the bottom of it ? Old Uncle Reuben. Of course, Captain Stickles was right about that. Come and see our rebellion, John. I will take only your word from you to keep silence, and most of all from your mother."

I promised that I would tell nobody.

"Meet me," he answered, "alone, of course, at the Wizard's Slough, at ten tomorrow morning."

I did as I was asked, and at first there was no sign of my uncle. It was a lonely desolate spot, and I was a little scared. Then at last Uncle Reuben appeared, on the other side of the pit, and beckoned me to him. Cautiously I edged my way round it and joined him.

I followed him to a great round hole in the ground, bratticed up with timber. "I will descend first," said Uncle Reuben. "When the bucket comes up again, follow me."

He climbed into a stout bucket, and was lowered into the shaft. I waited until it returned, and then I too descended.

On reaching the bottom, I was greeted by Uncle Reuben, and by a Cornishman named Carfax. It was a mine, and Uncle Ben led the way along a narrow passage, winding in and out, until we reached a great stone block or boulder, as large as my mother's oak wardrobe. Uncle Ben asked me to break it with the biggest of the sledgehammers, as they had been trying for a fortnight, and had not succeeded. After a few attempts I did so. Crashing and crushed, the great stone fell over and threads of sparkling gold appeared in the jagged sides of the breakage.

Soon afterwards we returned to the surface.

Lorna Gone Away

I told nobody but Lorna, whom I could trust as nobody else, about the mine near the Wizard's Slough, and when I mentioned the man Carfax, she thought at once of Gwenny, and how this man must be her father. We said nothing about it to Gwenny herself until we had discovered it to be the case, and the two of them were reunited after a separation of more than ten years.

Soon after this, I spent some days in Bodmin.

On reaching the farm once more, I knew that something had gone wrong there, and before long I found out what it was.

Lorna had gone to London, where she was awaited by her great uncle, some grand lord, who was appointed her guardian and master until she reached twenty-one.

The harvest was this year a heavy labour, and a thing for grumbling rather than gladness, and the house itself was dull and lonesome, for not only had my Lorna gone, but Annie too had left us, having married Tom Faggus. So apart from my mother, who was easily vexed, there was nobody I could talk to about my Lorna.

Soon afterwards, unable to bear it longer, I saddled my horse one morning and set off to visit Annie. She was very pleased to see me, and eased me into a better temper, so that I told her all about the strange history of Lorna and her departure and the small chance that remained to me of ever seeing my love again. Annie tried to comfort me, but there was little she could do. So I set off for Dulverton, and there encountered Ruth Huckaback.

I could not stay long, but before I left I told Ruth about Lorna and asked what I should do.

"Since she cannot send you token," Ruth spoke bravely, "and is not free to return to you, follow her, pay your court to her. Show her that you will not be forgotten, and she will not forget you."

The King is Dead

On Sunday, the eighth day of February 1685, we heard that the king, Charles the Second, had died.

We had been dressed in mourning for the dead king for three months and one week, as is customary, when rumours of disturbances, plottings and outbreak began to reach us. There was fighting in Scotland, ships being bought on the continent, and the buying of arms too in Devon and Somerset. We kept the beacon ready to give signals of a landing, but things went on almost as usual until the middle of June.

In June we had a visit from a man who was trying to win recruits for the army of the Duke of Monmouth, who was the Protestant son, although illegitimate, of the dead king. Monmouth was planning a rebellion against his uncle, King James, and for the next fortnight we were daily troubled with conflicting rumours – that the Duke had won a series of battles in the west country and that the men were flocking to his banner, and next that he was vanquished and put to flight, and on being caught had confessed that he was an imposter and a Catholic as bad as the king was.

I had intended that I would be kept out of these troubles, but one day at the start of July I came home to find Annie and the baby at the farm. Tom Faggus had joined the rebels, and Annie begged me to go after him.

I did not want to leave, fearing that the Doones would attack the farm, but Annie got from me the promise that if she could gain an assurance from

Counsellor Doone that he would leave us alone, then I would go and find Tom Faggus. I was surprised when she presented me with the assurance, written out and signed by the Counsellor, which she had obtained by throwing herself on his mercy in Glen Doone itself. The old man had, doubtless, other reasons for granting her this wish, but he liked Annie anyway, and had readily agreed. So I had no choice but to set out on my wild goose chase, not knowing which part of the country I was to go to.

Slaughter in the Marshes

It was not a happy journey, for I was bandied about from pillar to post, and sent to the following towns in succession: Bath, Frome, Wells, Wincanton, Glastonbury, Shepton, Bradford, Axbridge, Somerton and Bridgewater.

This last place was full of Monmouth's soldiers, half of whom had never been drilled nor had fired a gun.

I was woken up by the sounds of battle. I followed the sounds of battle out into the open marshes, where it was misty and where broad-water patches gleamed in the moonlight. All the time there was noise, sometimes of raging fight, others of a man dying.

After wandering for some time in this wilderness, I came upon a young man who knew the marshes well, and who was alone in the deserted camp of the

45

king's men. He led me to a broad open moor, where sedge grew, and which gave it its name — Sedgemoor. By now it was four o'clock in the morning, and by the pale light I could see all the ghastly scene of the aftermath of battle.

I dismounted and tried to give aid to the wounded and dying, and as I did so, I felt a horse's mouth close to my ear. Turning I saw Tom Faggus's horse, and followed her to where he lay. He had a great savage wound in his right side, from a pike-thrust or a musket ball. I bound it as well as I knew how, gave him some brandy and water, and the colour returned slightly to his pale face. He demanded to be placed on his horse, to make good his escape from the king's men, and I could do nothing else than help him. Left alone, I thought about my own situation – alone amid the remains of the rebel army, and if caught, likely to languish in some prison.

My fears were all but justified, for some rough soldiers of the king soon came up, and believing I was a rebel, were about to hang me from a tall tree, when Captain Jeremy Stickles rode up and demanded that I should be freed.

Suitable Devotion

On the advice of Jeremy Stickles, I decided that I would have to go straight to London to prove my innocence.

From many causes, it happened that I lived in London for five weeks before I could see Lorna. I heard of her from my landlord, a furrier, who told me that the Lady Lorna had been committed to the care of her mother's uncle, Earl Brandir of Lochawe. The Countess of Dugal had been the only child of the last Lord Lorne, whose sister had married Sir Ensor Doone, while he himself had married the sister of Earl Brandir. Lorna was now living with him, when she was not in attendance upon the queen, at his house in the village of Kensington.

He also told me that the king had given order that the doors of the palace of Whitehall should be thrown open, so that all who cared to see could watch him hearing mass. Lorna was there almost every Sunday, and the furrier, who had influence with a door-keeper, gained me admittance into the antechamber one Sunday.

It was a rich and colourful procession that passed me by as I stood at the back of a crowd of people. The king and queen were followed by their nobles, and among them was Lorna, dressed in purest white, with her eyes downcast. Would she see me, or would she not? As she passed, someone trod on the skirt of her dress and she raised her eyes and looked directly at me.

She made me a courtly bow, which was sweet and graceful when she did it, and the colour of her cheeks was as deep as that of my own. And the shining of her eyes was owing to an unpaid debt of tears.

47

Later that day, a servant came to me, bringing a letter from my love, saying that I was to go and see her, but naming no time. She loved me still.

I went to Kensington on Monday evening, and entered through the servants' door, where Gwenny Carfax let me in. She seemed not pleased to see me, but Lorna herself was delighted, and wept against my breast for joy. It appeared that she had written me letters, and had given them to Gwenny to send to me, but that Gwenny, thinking Lorna too good for me, had not sent them. Lorna was angry, but I knew it to be so. Then Lorna made me sit, and told me that the only difference there was between us was the fact that she had wealth to be envied by others, and I had not. And she hated her wealth, for there were only two people in the whole of London who did not either covet or despise her – one was Gwenny, and the other was the queen herself, who was fond of Lorna and too far above her to do either.

John is John no Longer

The old earl was very deaf, Lorna informed me, as a result of going out one cold night to look for his son, the same Alan Brandir who had spoken to Lorna years before, and been killed by Carver Doone for his pains. The earl still believed that his son was alive, and would return any day, and Lorna, who knew his fate, wanted to tell him what she knew —

but I forestalled her, knowing that news like that would send the old man to his grave in a few days.

The old earl used to keep all his money in a handsome pewter box, with a double lid and locks upon it, as well as his coat of arms. There was also a heavy chain, fixed to a staple in the wall, so that no one could carry off the box with the gold inside it. One evening towards September, I caught sight of two very villainous looking fellows watching the house from about a hundred yards away. Thinking there was bound to be mischief afoot, I lay in wait to see what the two villains did.

When it was almost pitch black, the attack came from the rear of the house, as I had expected. There were three of the villains, and I followed the men as far as Earl Brandir's bedroom, where they tried the door, knowing that he could hear nothing. The three men burst into the bedroom with a light and a crowbar and firearms. Two of them tried to break the locks on the pewter box, while the third had a gun to the earl's head and was demanding the key. The earl refused, saying that it was the property of his son Alan, and no one should have it, and prepared to die before he would yield.

On seeing this, I made my attack, and very soon had them bound up together. The constables were called, and the men appeared before the Justices in the morning.

That would have been an end of it, but for the fact that these men were greatly wanted by the king himself, for great offences they had done to him. He was very pleased with my work, and called me before him.

He asked me where he had seen me before.

"May it please Your Most Gracious Majesty," I said, "it was in the Royal Chapel."

Now I should have said the antechamber to the chapel, but I was confused by his presence. The king smiled, and said it was a great comfort to him to know that I was a Catholic too, and I did not dare contradict him.

The king asked of me what was my chief ambition, and I told him of my mother's wish for me to have a coat of arms, although this was not my wish. The king smiled and promised me that I should have a coat of arms, and then bade me kneel down. I did so, and before I knew what he was about, he said to me, "Arise, Sir John Ridd!"

Behaviour Not to be Borne

Beginning to be short of money, and wishing to show my mother my coat of arms, I returned home to Somerset, Lorna having intervened for me with the queen to make a trial unnecessary.

The Doones were still causing trouble, stealing livestock and grain to feed themselves with over the winter, and carrying off two maidens of the neighbourhood to be their wives. Before we had

finished meditating on this outrage, there followed another far worse, which turned our hearts sick.

After this, I was waylaid by the folk round about, and asked if I would be their leader against the Doones. I agreed, though I felt that it would be shameful to attack without warning, after they had behaved honourably to my family while I was away.

So, taking a white handkerchief to show I came unarmed, I went down to Glen Doone and asked to see Carver.

He made me wait, and then was surly and impolite with me. I commanded my temper, and told him that a vile and inhuman wrong had been done, but if he would make amends we would take no further action.

At this Carver Doone accused me of ingratitude. The Doones had kept faith with me, although I had stolen Lorna from them, he said, and now I repaid him by going into their township full of anger over a prank that some wayward Doones had played.

I admitted that I was grateful for their forbearance, but defended my stealing of Lorna, and tried to keep my temper.

"God knows better than thou or I how the balance hangs between us, Carver Doone," I finished. "Our day of reckoning is nigh."

"It is here, you fool!" he shouted treacherously, leaping aside. "Fire!"

At this the Doones began to fire their guns at me, but by swift running I escaped them, marvelling at their treachery.

A Long Account Settled

We enlisted the help of some yeomen from Barnstaple and Tiverton, and they brought with them heavy swords and short guns which would be very useful. Tom Faggus, who was now quite healed of his wound, joined us, and Uncle Ben came over with a band of stout warehousemen from Dulverton. He also promised us some of his miners from the Wizard's Slough, including Simon Carfax, Gwenny's father, whose grudge against the Doones was that they had stolen his daughter from him.

We devised a plan where some of the robbers would be deluded from home. A rumour was started that a large heap of gold was collected at the mine, and when this reached them, we sent Simon Carfax over to Glen Doone to demand an interview with the Counsellor by night, in which he would set forth a list of imaginary grievances against the mine owners. Then he offered to betray the whereabouts of the mine to the Doones on Friday night, on the understanding that he would take one quarter of it, and they would have the rest. Since the gold would be escorted by a lot of men, the Doones had to send at least a score of men.

All went according to plan, and on Friday night we attacked. One child I noticed especially, a fair and handsome little fellow, Carver Doone's son. The boy climbed on my back and rode with me. We set fire to the houses, and in the confusion, the women ran screaming that there were a hundred men attacking Glen Doone. Back came the Doone warriors. There were only a dozen or so of them, and my men wasted no time in opening fire on the men who had done them so much injury and wrong in the past.

Our blood was up, and that was a night of fire and slaughter and very long-harboured revenge. And before the daylight broke the next morning, the only Doones left alive were the Counsellor and Carver, and not one of their dwellings was left standing.

The Counsellor escaped through my doing, for I had sworn before the battle that I would not have him harmed. In the thick of fighting, I had seen him scuttling away on all fours towards one of the small gates that led out of Glen Doone. I fetched him up short, whereupon he flattered and begged me, in most cowardly fashion, to spare his life. I told him that I would, in return for two things. The first was that he would tell me who slew my father – it was

Carver, as I had thought all along. Secondly, I wished to have back in my trust Lorna's necklace, which he had stolen from her. He told me that Carver had taken that too, but I did not believe him, and indeed found it in his pocket. Then I let him go, and what became of him I do not know.

Carver Doone was left to wander, homeless, foodless and desperate on Exmoor, having sworn vengeance on me on the deadliest of oaths.

How to Get Out of Chancery

The next thing that happened to me was that Lorna came back, in wonderful health and spirits. She ran about the rooms of the farmhouse, and all the house was full of brightness.

Upon Judge Jeffreys' return from the Bloody Assizes, where he had hung five thousand people, he had pleased the king so greatly with his account of the poor folk's agonies that the king had made him Chancellor, and Lorna's fate hung upon him, for at the same time the old earl died.

The Lady Lorna Dugal appeared to Lord Chancellor Jeffreys so wealthy a ward of court that some money must come his way, and he visited her. She plied him with fine wines, and held out such golden promise of a heap of money which would come his way, that he had given her his consent to her marriage with Sir John Ridd, upon condition that the king's consent was obtained. The king gave his consent, on condition that on coming of age Lorna should pay a heavy fine to the Crown and devote a fixed portion of her estate to the promotion of the Catholic faith. However, since King James the Second was driven out of his kingdom before this arrangement could come into effect, that agreement was pronounced improper and invalid.

Blood Upon the Altar

Everything was settled smoothly, and without any fear or fuss, that Lorna might find end of troubles and myself of eager waiting, with the help of Parson Bowden and the good wishes of two counties.

Lorna's dress was of pure white, and as simple as need be, except for perfect loveliness. I was almost afraid to look at her, except when each of us said, "I will," and then each dwelled upon the other.

Her eyes told me such a tale of hope and faith and devotion that I was almost amazed. The clearest eyes, the loveliest, the most loving eyes — the sound of a shot rang through the church, and those eyes were dim with death.

Lorna fell across my knees when I was going to kiss her, as the bridegroom is allowed to do; I lifted her up, but it was no good. The only sign of life remaining was a red drip of blood.

Of course, I knew who had done it. There was but

one man who could have done such a thing. I laid my wife in my mother's arms, leaped upon our best horse, with bridle, but no saddle, and set off after Carver Doone.

I had no weapon of any sort so, unarmed, dressed in my bridal coat, red with the blood of the bride, I went forth to find out whether there is a God of justice.

At furious speed I came upon Black Barrow Down, and there a furlong or so in front of me on a great black horse rode Carver Doone.

I knew his strength, and that he was armed with a pistol, but I had no more doubt of killing the man in front of me than a cook has of cooking a dead chicken.

I followed him over the long moor, reckless whether I was seen or not. But only once did he look back, and then I was beside a rock with a reedy swamp behind me. He had something on the horse before him, something which needed care.

He turned towards Wizard's Slough, and as he did so he turned to see me not a hundred yards behind . him. Then I saw that what he had with him was his little son Ensie, whom I had looked after. Seeing me, the child cried out and stretched his arms out to me, for the face of his father frightened him.

Carver Doone bared his teeth at the sight of me, and turned his horse to plunge into the black ravine leading to the Wizard's Slough. I followed my enemy carefully, steadily, even leisurely, for I had him where no escape might be. There was a gnarled oak tree hanging from the crag above me. Rising from my horse, I caught a branch and tore it from its socket, to use as a weapon.

Carver Doone turned the corner suddenly, and came upon the black and evil bog. He reined back his horse sharply, but rode on, hoping to find a way round its side. There is such a way, but he could not feel it. I placed my horse across his way, and with the branch of the oak I hit his mount hard upon the head, so that all three, man, boy and horse, came down.

Carver Doone was stunned for a moment, and I leaped to the ground. The child Ensie ran to me in terror, and very gently I bade him go back round the corner and pick flowers for the pretty lady. I might have killed Carver there and then, but that would have been foul play.

I think he felt his time had come. A paleness came on his cheeks, and seeing this I offered him first chance. In this I was too generous, for he caught me round the waist, and I felt my rib break.

I grasped his arm, and tore the muscle out of it. Then I took him by the throat, as he had gone for mine, and in vain he strained and writhed, dashing his fist into my face and flinging himself upon me with gnashing jaws. Beneath the iron of my strength I had him helpless in two minutes.

"I will not harm thee more," I cried. "Carver Doone, thou art beaten: admit it, and thank God for it, and repent thyself!"

It was all too late. The black bog had him by the feet; the sucking of the ground drew on him like the thirsty lips of death. I gave a mighty leap to escape the engulfing grave of slime. He fell back, then tossed his arms to heaven, and they were black to the elbow. The glare of his eyes was ghastly. I could only gaze and pant while, joint by joint, he sank from sight.

When the child came back, the only sign of his father was a dark brown bubble upon a new-formed patch of blackness. I picked up the child and rode for home. By the time I reached the farm, I was weak and the thought of Lorna's death, like a heavy knell, was tolling in the belfry of my brain.

Give Away the Grandeur

"I have killed him," I said to my mother, "even as he has killed Lorna. Let me see my wife, Mother. Let me see my dead one and then die."

All the women fell away from me except Ruth. One little hand of hers stole into mine, as she said softly, "She is not dead, John, but you must not see her now. The sight of you in this sad plight would kill her."

"Is there any chance for her?" I asked.

"God in Heaven knows, John. Come and be healed yourself."

I obeyed her like a child. I learned that if it had not been for Ruth, Lorna must have died at once, but from the moment I left her Ruth had come forward and taken charge of everyone. She had staunched the blood, and taken out the bullet from the vile wound in my Lorna's side. She had sponged Lorna's side and her forehead, and had poured wine between Lorna's teeth, so that she had given a little flutter in the throat, and a sigh.

But for hours and days she lay at the very verge of death, kept alive by nothing but the care, the skill and the watchfulness of Ruth. Lorna recovered long before I did.

I lay close to death. I believed that Lorna was dead, while these rogues were lying to me, and I seemed quite fit to go to heaven for I had no wish to live.

One day I was sitting in my bedroom, for the doctor was coming to bleed me again that day.

Presently a little knock came at the door. I tried to rise, thinking it to be the doctor, but it was Ruth, who had never once come to visit me. She was gaily dressed, and I was sorry for her bad manners while my Lorna lay dead.

"Can you receive visitors, John Ridd?" she asked, running to me, and then she spotted the basin, and asked what it was for.

"That basin," I said, "is for the doctor to bleed me."

Ruth was outraged. She flung the basin to the floor and stamped upon it, demanding that I should be bled no more, for it was that which was killing me. I promised, on this excitement, to leave my curing entirely to her.

She laughed, and said that she would now save

my life as she had saved Lorna's, and I was very puzzled by this. Ruth then ran out of the room, and came back followed by my Lorna, who ran to me and threw herself into my arms, and I felt my life come back as she did so.

Little more have I to tell. The doctor was turned out at once, and Ruth took charge, and I slowly became well again, nursed by good food and a darling wife. Lorna never tired of sitting with me, and even now she never tires of being with me, talking of these adventures which took place.

Lorna has great stores of money, but we never use it, for she prefers to live simply and I love her the better for that. I believe that gives away half the grandeur, and keeps the other half for the children.

Tom Faggus settled down and renounced his old, bad ways. Little Ensie was sent to my old school, at my expense. He looks upon me as his father.

Ruth Huckaback is not married yet, although on Uncle Ben's death she inherited all his property except £2,000 which he left to me.

Of Lorna I will not speak, for it is unseemly to boast. Yet her beauty grows year by year together with goodness, kindness and true happiness, and above all with loving. And if I wish to pay her out for something very dreadful — as may happen once or twice when we become too happy — I bring her to forgotten sadness and to me for cure of it, by the two words, "Lorna Doone."